TROLL'S
CAVE

TROLL'S WOOD

Troll's Crossing

THE
ASH GROVE

PUFFER'S POND

Woodkin Hollow

THE BEECH GROVE

Fairy Wings

A STORY BY LAUREN MILLS

WITH PAINTINGS BY

LAUREN MILLS & DENNIS NOLAN

Little, Brown and Company

Boston   New York   Toronto   London

We wish to thank the Society for
the Preservation of Fairies:
Evie, George, Rebecca, Katie,
Danny, Lynn, Maria, Susan,
and the Schramers

For Evie
love,
Mom & Dad

Text copyright © 1995 by Lauren A. Mills
Illustrations copyright © 1995 by Lauren A. Mills and Dennis Nolan
Calligraphy by Julian Waters

First Edition

Library of Congress Cataloging-in-Publication Data
Mills, Lauren A.
 Fairy wings / a story by Lauren Mills with paintings by Lauren Mills
and Dennis Nolan—1st ed.
  p.   cm.
 Summary: Although she is looked down on because she doesn't have
any wings, Fia manages to save the other fairies in the Fairy
Kingdom when a wicked Troll attacks.
 ISBN 0-316-57397-3
 [1. Fairy tales.] I. Title.
PZ8.M635Far 1995
[E]—dc20   92-37168

10 9 8 7 6 5 4 3 2

Published simultaneously in Canada by Little, Brown & Company (Canada) Limited
Paintings done in graphite and watercolor.
Color separations made by New Interlitho Italia S.p.A.
Text set in Galliard by Typographic House.
Printed and bound by New Interlitho Italia S.p.A.

Printed in Italy

Once, when the trees and flowers grew as they pleased, there lived a host of the tiniest, most delicate fairies. Every spring, the air hummed with the sound of fairies fluttering from blossom to blossom to preen their gossamer wings for the grand May Dance. All the fairies prized their wings above anything else—all but little Fia, that is, for she was the one fairy born without wings.

Now, Fia's wingless condition was no easy burden to bear for her seven older sisters, whose lovely wings were spoken of in far-off lands.

"We do not blame Fia for having no wings, but her earthy behavior is a disgrace to us all!" Violet said to their mother one morning while the sisters were polishing each other's wings. "We were not invited to the High Tea of Elderberry Vine again this month, and I am certain it is because Fia was recently spotted parading through a mud puddle with that slimy frog!"

"And last month," added Rose, "she frightened our friends out of their hammocks when she rode through the reeds on that horrid rat!"

"And the month before that," chirped in Pansy, "she spoiled our party when she soared over us on that nasty, noisy crow!"

"Perhaps if you would invite Fia to some of these affairs, she would not bother you so," said their mother.

"Bees' knees, Mother!" exclaimed Daisy. "Why should we invite Fia to anything when she insists on cavorting with those loathsome animals?"

"Those animals are the *only* friends Fia has," scolded their mother.

Fia's sisters bowed their heads with shame. "We're sorry, Mother," said Aster. "It's just that we heard that the royal family *itself* might join our May Dance this year!" She lowered her voice. "Now, what sort of impression will we make with Fia there?"

"I don't think you need to worry about little Fia," their mother reassured them. "She rarely bothers with fairy dances. Now, come, my sweet blossoms, let us go dry our wings under the willow tree."

That same morning, Fia had fashioned a tiny boat from the discarded eggshell of a goose, and using a holly leaf as her oar, she paddled to the center of Frog's Pond.

"Frog, it works!" she cried. "Rat! Crow! Come see my boat!"

Rat sluggishly stuck his head out from the brambles and yawned. Crow flew overhead and dropped an elderberry in front of Fia. She laughed, paddling over to it, and batted it through the water. "This is great fun, Rat," she said as her egg boat bobbed to and fro. "You ought to try—" But before she could finish, Rat quickly disappeared.

"Oh, Rat! The water's not so bad. You really ought to try it. There is so much more to life than living in a hole in the ground."

"*Gullumph*," came a noise from Frog as he gulped down a fly.

"Aagh!" shouted Fia, shutting her eyes. "I wish you wouldn't do that in front of me, Frog."

Just then, Fia heard a rustling in the leaves. She expected Rat to emerge, but instead a stranger appeared—a fairy boy!

Fia kept silent, for fear he was of the mind to tease her, but the boy exclaimed, "How clever! You've made a boat! Might I have a try?"

In a wink, Fia was at the bank, eagerly handing him her paddle. But the fairy boy took a step away from her in dismay. "Oh, my! You... you... haven't any wings!" he stammered.

Fia snatched back her paddle and was about to run away when the boy stopped her.

"Please excuse me. That must have sounded rude. I've just never seen a fairy without wings, and well, oh, how unlucky....I am truly sorry," he said in a kind voice.

"No need to be sorry," said Fia shortly. "*I'm* not. It is you wingèd fairies I pity, always having to mind that you don't tear your wings!"

The fairy boy laughed. "You *are* lucky, then! As a matter of fact, I tore *my* wing on a thorn, and I can't fly again until it is mended."

Fia examined his wing. "Oh, I can mend that," she said.

"Well, since it is already torn..." said the fairy boy, looking at Fia's boat with longing.

"Here!" said Fia, handing him her paddle once more. "You try this boat. I'll fetch the other half of the eggshell." And in no time at all, the two had made up a wild game full of splashes and shrieks as they batted the floating elderberry through the rippling water.

After a bit, Fia said, "Come. I'll show you to my teahouse. I can mend your wing there." She led the fairy boy through the tall reeds.

"What is your name?" she asked. "Mine is Fia."

"Fia," he repeated. "Yes, that suits you. You can just call me Kip."

"Will you have time for a cup of mint tea, Kip? If you say yes, you will be the first fairy ever to have tea with me," said Fia, beginning to worry that he might say no.

"I can think of nothing better, Fia," he answered.

Now, what Fia called her teahouse was not the kind found in the upper quarters of the Elderberries—one with velvet-and-lace cushions, a china tea set, and jeweled lamps. No, Fia had made this teahouse herself, from grapevine twigs, leaves, moss, and so forth.

Fia rummaged through her cupboard and found some spider's silk, which she nimbly threaded through a rabbit's whisker. She wove the thread back and forth through Kip's wing so that one could hardly tell that it had ever been torn. As she finished, they heard the distant sound of wind pipes.

Kip sighed. "My parents are calling me. This has been more fun than...well, more fun than I've ever had." Then, with a quick turn of his head, he stole a kiss from Fia and flew off.

Fia stared after him. Even her own sisters had never kissed her! Then, glancing down, she saw a tiny note tucked under a mint leaf napkin. It was an invitation to the May Dance—with Fia's name scribbled on it! She ran home, clutching the invitation the whole way.

W hy is the May Dance going to be held in the Ash Grove?" Pansy was asking her father as Fia arrived home. "Isn't that dangerously close to Troll's Wood?"

"'Tis the Queen's wish," he replied, "so that she may better see all your pretty wings reflecting in the glassy water of Puffer's Pond. Come hither, little Fia, and sit next to me. My, you're out of breath!"

Fia snuggled close to her father on the soft sofa of milkweed down.

"How do you know all this, Father?" asked Heather.

"The Queen told me. 'We wish to arrange the marriage of our son, Prince Hyacinth,' she said, 'and I've heard it said you have seven beautiful daughters.'" Suddenly their father looked down at Fia and quickly corrected himself. "Eight. The Queen said *eight* beautiful daughters." Fia looked up at her father and smiled.

"And then what did the Queen say, Father?" Marigold prompted.

"She said, 'Please be sure your daughters are all present at the dance, for the fairy maiden with the most beautiful wings will be my son's bride and the future Queen of Fairy Wood.'"

Fia clapped her hands. "One of my sisters will surely be Queen!"

Fia's sisters all laughed and said, "What a dear little sister we have! We will tell you all about the dance when we come home."

"Oh, but I am *going!*" exclaimed Fia, waving her invitation over her head. "Kip, my new friend, has invited me!"

"Kip! Who is Kip?" the sisters all chirped frantically. "Is he an ugly toad? A grasshopper?" they asked in unkindly voices.

"Kip happens to be a very nice fairy boy!" retorted Fia, standing with her hands on her hips. They could tease *her,* but she would not allow them to make fun of her new friend.

"Wherever did *you* meet a fairy boy?" asked Daisy.

"He came out of the brambles when I was boating in a goose egg, and he joined me in a game. He was quite good at it!"

"Hhumph! A goose egg! Brambles! He must be one of those traveling tramps! You want nothing to do with him, Fia. You ought to be a good little sister and stay home," Violet replied.

"Yes, stay home and play with Froggie," added Daisy.

Fia's eyes filled with tears. She shook her head no and began to finger her invitation.

"Father, you talk to her. She'll listen to you," implored Rose.

"I have *eight* beautiful daughters," said their father sternly, "and eight daughters are going to this dance."

Fia and her mother spent the next several days making Fia's dress. It was woven from the finest milkweed down and embroidered with silken threads dyed from raspberries and mustard flowers. It was the loveliest dress in the glen, and Fia's sisters grew quite jealous.

On the morning of the dance, Fia sat happily embroidering the last bit of lace to her collar, when Violet landed on a nearby stem.

"Fia," she said saucily, "I really don't know why Mother wasted precious time over *you*. Only the seven of us will matter to the Queen."

"Well, perhaps *I* will matter to someone else," responded Fia.

"Don't be stupid! Do you really believe that a fairy boy would want to be seen at a dance with *you*? Just think about *that*, Fia!" said her sister haughtily as she flew away.

For the rest of the day, Fia could think of nothing but her sister's words. And by afternoon she was certain that Violet was right.

Just before dusk, the old oak hollow was abuzz with fairies dressing for the grand May Dance. But Fia was nowhere to be seen. Her mother said, "I can't find her anywhere, and I've searched all the likely places."

"That's not how to find Fia, Mother," said Marigold. "You must look in all the *un*likely places. Try under toadstools, down mole holes, in old beehives." Fia's sisters all laughed.

"You mustn't laugh. I'm worried," said their mother. "Last night the Troll was seen just across the river."

A little voice from the window ledge said, "I'm right here, Mother."

"Fia! You must hurry! The pipes will be sounding soon!"

"I'm sorry, Mother, but I shan't be going. The wind has stolen my dress and flung it into the brambles." Fia neglected to mention that she had thrown her dress to the wind on purpose.

"Anyway, I no longer wish to go to the dance. I have other plans," Fia said staunchly, trying to keep her voice from quivering. "Good luck, sisters!" She scurried down a branch and was quickly out of sight.

At twilight the sound of the pipes echoed through the woods. The fairies flew from their hollows, all carried by their freshly polished wings, which flickered as brightly as a sprinkling of tiny stars. Fia gazed longingly at the glowing procession of fairies floating across the glen. She would never be one of them, she thought. For the first time, the sadness of having no wings filled her whole being until she shook with sobs.

Soon she heard the cawing of Crow. She looked up at her friend and said angrily, "Don't you see, Crow? I didn't care before, but now it *matters* that I don't have wings!"

Crow landed next to her and cawed again, hopping on one foot and then the other in a huff.

"Yes, Crow, I know I have *you,* and *you* have wings," said Fia. "But there are other reasons for a fairy to have wings than for flying. Sometimes it is just for show that matters."

Crow flew off but soon returned with Fia's beautiful dress in his beak. Fia smiled at his kindness. "If you insist, Crow, I'll wear it, but only for you." She slipped on her dress, brushed her hair till it shone, and began to dance lightly on the moss, pretending that she and Kip were flying together at the May Dance.

Fia was startled out of her dream by Rat, Crow, and Frog, who beckoned her to the edge of the bank, where, to her delight, she saw an ornately decorated float, fit for a queen. On a lily pad was a throne of blossoms, grapevine twigs, and milkweed down. Stretching out from the sides were lacy camellia leaves and drops of dew and nectar, all of which, in the moonlight, looked curiously like a pair of splendid fairy wings.

Frog jumped into the water, ready to pull the float down the river. Fia looked at her dear friends, who had worked so desperately hard to please her. "It is for them that I will go," she thought as she stepped onto the lily pad and up onto the throne.

Rat followed the float along the riverbank. Crow soon lost interest and cawed one last "good night" as he flew off to his perch for a good night's sleep.

"Good night, Crow, and thank you!" Fia called out merrily, but as she did, a large dark shadow passed over her and spread across the riverbank. Nervously, she twisted about but saw nothing.

"Oh, me, I have the jitters. I'm sure it was only a cloud crossing the moon. We must think only happy thoughts tonight," she murmured, and began to hum a cheerful tune while Frog kicked in rhythm.

As they rounded the bend in the river, they could hear chimes, harps, and flutes. A lovely chorus of tiny fairy voices that sounded like the tinkling of bells called out, "Hail, Prince Hyacinth!" Fia's heart beat faster as Frog swam closer to the bank.

"Not so fast, Frog. I don't want to be seen. I just want to look," said Fia. But Frog kept swimming, his legs never missing a beat.

A pleasant minuet had begun. The fairies danced along the ground in a circle. One side rose above the grass, then the other, until the whole ring of fairies was spinning in the air. Fia was breathless merely from watching the enchanting spectacle.

As the fairy ring returned to earth again, Fia heard a great deal of murmuring. Frog had reached the bank, and now all heads were turned toward her!

They all began to speak at once. "Who is she? Is she a princess? She must be—look at her exotic throne. And those *wings,* they are the most extraordinary I've ever seen!"

Fia gasped. "Frog, take me away!" she whispered. Rat had begun to pull Fia's throne up onto the bank when two coachmen brushed him aside, then carried the throne themselves right through the ring and set Fia down in front of the King and Queen!

All the fairies moved in closer without a word. Even Fia's own family did not recognize her.

Fia knew it was only proper to curtsy before the King and Queen, yet she dared not, lest they see she had no wings.

Suddenly the Prince stood, taking Fia's hands and bowing before her.

"Fia, you're trembling. Perhaps you would feel better if we danced?"

Fia found her voice. "I-I cannot," she stammered as she looked into the Prince's eyes. To her amazement, she saw that it was Kip!

"Kip, you are the Prince?" Fia whispered.

Kip smiled. "Do you like the chair I sent down to you?"

"*You* sent the chair?" Fia exclaimed.

"Yes. I made it myself…but without those magnificent wings attached."

"Oh, these….I believe my friends added them for me. I am sorry, Kip, I really should not be here," Fia whispered, glancing at the crowd.

Kip snapped his fingers, and the music began. "Come, Fia," he said softly. "Dance with me. My wings can carry us both."

Fia stood, and Kip whisked her quickly into his arms, twirling her around the ring of fairies and up into the air, until Fia felt like she was flying herself! But Kip was not quick enough to keep everyone, especially the King and Queen, from noticing that Fia had no wings.

"What is this outrage?" cried the Queen. "Who has brought this wingless creature here?"

The King clapped his hands for the music to stop. Kip reluctantly brought Fia back to earth, and though the Queen was dizzy with anger, Kip ceremoniously bowed to Fia.

"Thank you so much, Fia. I apologize for my parents," he said.

"Do not be sorry, Kip. I shall never forget tonight...nor you. Now I must go," she said with tears in her eyes. Rat rushed up to her and she gratefully climbed onto his back, clutching the scruff of his neck.

Turning to the silent crowd of fairies, Rat lifted his nose in the air with a loud snort, then swaggered down to the bank, where Frog awaited them. Without hesitation, Rat stepped onto the lily pad, shoving off from the bank with his hind leg. Fia patted Rat's head, which was beginning to shudder with the fear of the deep water all about him.

The music began to play once more, and Fia's heart was filled with the most sadness she had ever known. She never would have turned to look back if it had not been for the terrible sound of screaming fairies.

"Oh, no!" Fia cried in horror. The Troll had come! He was hairy and grotesque, and he carried an enormous net. The wings of the fairies shone so brightly that the Troll had no trouble capturing them, every last one.

Fia watched helplessly as the Troll trudged off, laughing wickedly with his net of squirming, screeching fairies.

Frog swam in frenzied circles, frightened and confused. Rat wavered from side to side, trying to avoid the water that splashed up around his ankles.

"Stop, Frog!" commanded Fia. "We must find a way to save them. Swim to the Beech Grove, where the woodkins live. They can help us."

When they reached the bank, Fia said to Rat, "Go wake Crow, and tell him where to find us. Hurry!" Rat raced out of sight.

Frog and Fia could hear music coming from one particular beech tree. "Wait for me at the bank," said Fia. Frog looked at her with worried eyes.

"Don't worry, Frog, the woodkins won't harm me." Fia said, and kissed him on the nose.

No one heard Fia's knock above all the ruckus, so she let herself in and wandered down a crooked tunnel filled with dead leaves and spiderwebs. She entered a great hall where woodkins were singing and dancing everywhere. One by one they took notice of Fia, and drums, banjos, spoons, and singing all stopped.

"Eh, eh, eh, what perty litt'l fairy tyke 'as stooped so low as to visit we miser'ble ol' woodkins?" said one of the elders. The woodkins laughed, and someone pushed Fia to the center of the room.

"Stop it, Daffer! Stop it, all of you!" scolded a little woman Fia recognized. "It's our friend, Fia, the wingless fairy. She 'as never taunted ye, so ye shall not taunt her!"

"Please, I've come to beg for your help," pleaded Fia in a quivering voice. "The Troll came to our May Dance tonight and snatched up everyone. Please help me save them!"

The room was silent. And then came one snicker after another.

"Now, let me get this straight," said Daffer. "All ye fairies gone out o' the wood? No more fairies stealing our honey? No more fairies dropping nuts on our heads? No more teasin'? No more tauntin'? I say good riddance to ye fairies!" They all cheered and banged spoons.

Fia searched the room frantically. "Won't *any*one help me?"

Daffer strode over to her and said, "Listen, Fia. Your own folk haven't been none too kind to you, either. There's no use riskin' yer life fer 'em, now is there? You come live with us. How about it? You could marry young Buckthorne over there."

Fia looked in the direction Daffer was pointing and saw Buckthorne taking off his sock and blowing his nose in it. She began to pale.

"Thank you, kindly, but I must go now and find the troll," she said, backing away. The little woodkin woman brashly moved the burly woodkins aside with her stick and led Fia out the passageway.

"Isadora!" Daffer yelled after them. "You know what luck befalls a woodkin who helps a fairy!" Still Isadora bustled up the passageway.

She turned to Fia when they reached the open air. "The woodkins aren't willing to risk their lives nor their luck for the fairies. But ye helped my children when they were sick, so I will help ye the best I can." She scrambled over a root, and a moment later reappeared. "Here is a cart and some blankets for yer journey."

"You are kind," said Fia. "But how am I to save them with just these and three animals? I don't even know where the Troll lives!"

"Hush, girl, and I will tell you a riddle:

> *The old Troll's home is a ratlike place.*
> *His greed is a froglike thing.*
> *But when Crow wakes, Troll hides his face,*
> *Or gather he moss, not wing.*

"There, now, that is all I can do. So be off with you!" said Isadora, tapping Fia with her stick before disappearing.

Fia pushed the cart as fast as she could to the bank, where, to her relief, sat Frog, Rat, and Crow. She told her friends the riddle, but they were none too pleased to be likened to the Troll.

"'The old Troll's home is a ratlike place,'" repeated Fia, looking at Rat. "It must be a dark *hole* in the ground...a very large hole...a cave! And the only place a cave could be is at the side of that mountain.

"I must get there right away. Crow, if I ride on your back, will you be strong enough to carry Rat and Frog in this cart?"

Crow nodded sleepily, and Fia hoped he was awake enough to understand what he had agreed to. Rat and Frog jumped into the cart, and Fia climbed onto Crow's back.

"Off to the mountain!" she said, and away they flew by the lingering light of the moon.

At last, Fia saw what she was searching for. "There, Crow, see, down there!" she said. They circled lower and lower as they watched the Troll disappear into a hole in the mountainside.

The foursome circled above the mouth of the cave. Crow shivered while Rat and Frog hid beneath the blankets. "Come, friends, we can't turn back now," urged Fia, shaking a bit herself.

They entered the cave and flew down a dismal hallway. Along the rock walls were lit torches, and holding them were hideous-looking trolls. At first Fia thought they were alive, but then she realized they were only stone, covered with hairy moss.

They landed unseen in the dark corner of an eerie chamber. Below them, one candle lit the table where the bundle of fairies lay. Their wails and cries echoed through the cave, as did the *scrape-scrape* of the Troll sharpening his knife. With slobber running down his chin, the Troll shook his shaggy head from side to side. The monstrous shadow he cast hovered on the ceiling above them, causing the four to shudder.

Fia heard her sister Rose cry out, "Oh, please, Troll, don't eat us!"

The Troll's thundering laughter filled the cave. "Eat you? Ha! Ha! Ha! Fairies taste *bad!* Too many little bones."

"Then what is it you want?" demanded Kip.

The Troll leaned toward them and smiled, showing his ugly yellow teeth in the candlelight. "Why, I just want your wings...pretty things for my collection," he said. And with a self-satisfied growl, he went back to sharpening his knife.

The fairies moaned and wailed. "But without our wings we are nothing," lamented Violet. "We will be just like Fia!"

"And play with frogs? I'd rather die!" sobbed Daisy.

Frog scowled. "Never mind them, Frog," said Fia. "They just don't know what they're missing." Just then a fly buzzed by Frog, who did not waste the opportunity to stick out his tongue and snatch it.

"Frog! How could you be greedy for flies at a time like this?" scolded Fia. Then she remembered the second part of the riddle. " 'His greed is a froglike thing,' " she said. "He's greedy for things that *fly*. If only I had *wings*, I could *fly* in front of the Troll and distract him while the others escape." She began feverishly taking bits and pieces off the cart Isadora had given her: grapevine tendrils, leaf stems, threads from the blankets. Frog and Rat made no move to help her.

"Well, what's wrong? You've made wings for me *before!*" she implored. So Rat gave her one of his whiskers to sew with, and Frog, with his clever tongue, unhinged a spiderweb full of dew drops. "We're almost ready, but we could use some of these," Fia said, plucking out some of Crow's most tender tufts of feathers. Poor Crow had been sound asleep, so of course, he awoke with a start.

"Sshh," whispered Fia to Crow. "It must be nearly morning by now, anyway, Crow." Then she remembered the last part of the riddle.

" 'But when Crow wakes, Troll hides his face,' " she murmured. "Crow usually wakes when the sun rises...so it is the *sun* that the Troll must hide from." Fia looked back at the stone trolls in the hallway....
" 'Or gather he moss, not wing!' Of course! Now I know what I must do!

"Oh, no, he's grabbed Kip!" cried Fia. "Let's go!"

Crow rose, lifting Rat by the scruff of his neck while Fia, with her wings, in place, hung on to Rat's tail and Frog clung to Fia's feet.

Crow gave a piercing caw, flapped his big black wings, and flew up and behind the Troll. Then Frog heroically jumped down the back of the Troll's tunic, startling him so that he dropped his knife and Kip.

And then there was Fia, with her handmade wings, swinging back and forth in front of the Troll's face. Never had the Troll been so tempted, and his greed for those strange and wonderful wings overtook him. He swatted and he batted, but, try as he might, he could not capture Fia, for Crow carefully kept her just beyond his reach.

Fia was in danger of losing her grip, but she urged Crow to lead the greedy Troll outside. The Troll followed them through the doorway. Fia hung on with her last bit of strength as they flew around and around, and then—a ray of sunlight hit the Troll. He stopped and turned to stone, his greedy arm reaching out in vain forever more.

In no time, Kip had cut the net, and all the fairies rushed out of the cave in one swarm, buzzing with cheers for Fia. "She will go down in history!" exclaimed the King.

"There is no other like her," stated the Queen.

"And she is our sister!" shouted Fia's sisters, hoping everyone would take notice of them.

All were flying about and dancing in the air, but Kip, alone, found Fia with Rat and Crow sitting on the foot of the stone Troll. Fia had tears streaming down her cheeks.

"What is it?" asked Kip, with his arm around Fia.

"Frog is gone," she sobbed. "He has turned to stone with the Troll! Oh, my dear, dear Frog. There will never be another like you!"

"*Gullumph!*" they heard as another fly was swallowed... by none other than Frog!

"Oh, Frog! That is the sweetest sound I've ever heard!" cried Fia as she rushed through the grasses to embrace her friend.

The rest of the fairies circled around the rescue team and sang and danced in the air. Then a beautiful palanquin was made for Fia, Kip, Rat, and Frog to ride in. It was carried with ribbons by Fia's sisters. And Crow, well, Crow excused himself from the ceremonious flight to Fairy Wood and flew straight home to his own perch to catch up on the sleep he so well deserved. And all the way back, Kip's parents spoke to Fia's about a wedding... "come next May."

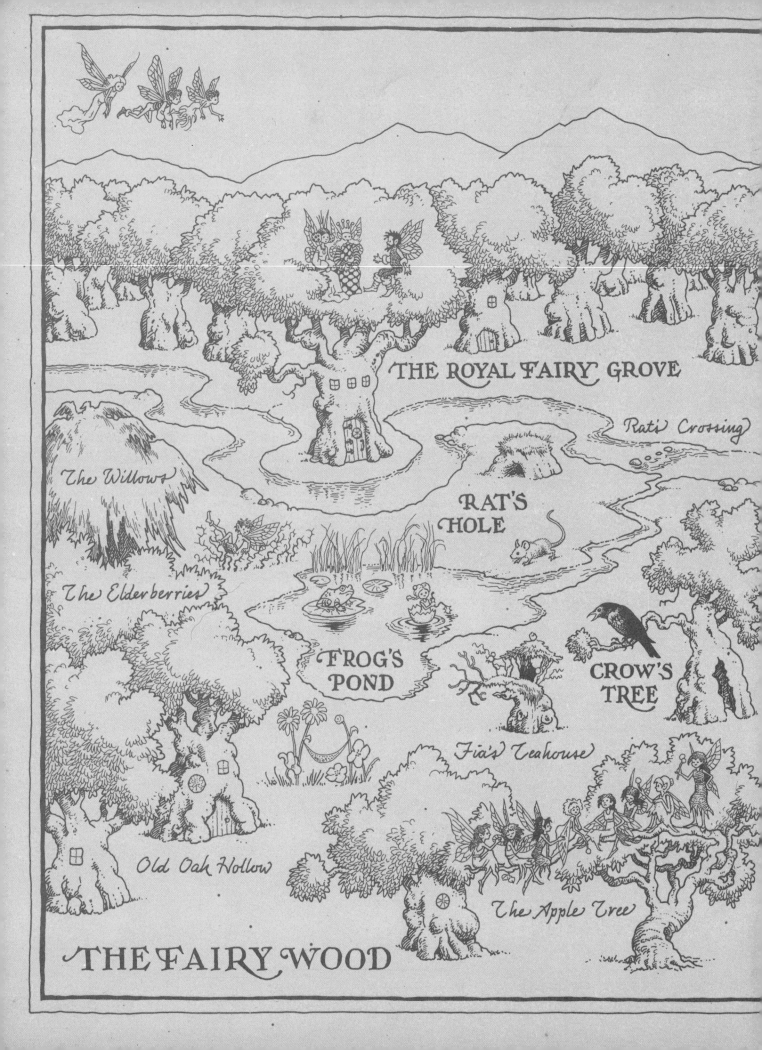

THE ROYAL FAIRY GROVE

Rats Crossing

The Willows

RAT'S HOLE

The Elderberries

FROG'S POND

CROW'S TREE

Fia's Teahouse

Old Oak Hollow

The Apple Tree

THE FAIRY WOOD